EMBRACING FATE

Also by Alexandria Blaelock

SHORT STORY COLLECTIONS
The Histories of Hayward Hall
Lovelorn, Lovestruck and Love at First Sight
Common or Garden Variety Heroes
Case Files of the Wilkinson Detective Agency
Unavoidable Fates
Christmas Travesties
Five Faces of Felicia Clarke
Little Place Called Home
Security Directorate Dossiers v. 1.
Security Directorate Dossiers v. 2.

FICTION
That Love Nonsense
Taipan vs Brown
The Ghost and Ms Cox
Friends Like That
Weaving the Wildwood
Wolf vs Orb

MS BLAELOCK'S BOOKS
Stress Free Dinner Parties
Signature Wardrobe Planning
Holistic Personal Finance
Minimally Viable Housekeeping
Planning a Life Worth Living

PICTURE BOOKS
Australia Felix

SELECTED SHORT STORIES
Alma's Grace
Blood and Bloody Profanity
Cancelled by the Cartel
Dingo Hunting
Honoris Virilis Respectu
Mince Pie Mystery
Remains of Christmas

EMBRACING FATE

A FATES SHORT STORY

ALEXANDRIA BLAELOCK

BlueMere Books
MELBOURNE, AUSTRALIA

For permission requests, please contact
enquiries@bluemerebooks.com.

Ordering Information:
Discounts are available on quantity purchases. For details, contact orders@bluemerebooks.com.

Embracing Fate/Alexandria Blaelock
paperback ISBN: 978-1-925749-83-0
digital ISBN: 978-1-925749-84-7

Book Layout © BookDesignTemplates.com
Cover Art © Warm_Tail licenced from Shutterstock.com

EMBRACING FATE

When Susan Grant died, Agatha was there; right next to the bed.

Susan was stuck in the air-conditioned hospice room, slipping in and out of consciousness.

Agatha knew she was aware of the cold, and the familiar smells of antiseptic and the chemicals they used to clean the machines.

Though she may not have been fully aware of the full extent of the room's greyness; grey lino on the floor, grey paint on the walls, and grey laminated cupboards on the walls.

Even some kind of weird grey on grey abstract painting on the wall facing the bed.

Agatha wondered if the greyness was sup-posed to ease the transition between life and death, though anyone who wasn't dying when they came in would certainly be when they walked out.

In fact, everyone was dying.

Day by day drawing closer to their deaths.

Except her of course, given she controlled the date and means of everyone's death.

Agatha put her tiny posy of pale blue forget-me-nots in a plastic cup from the water dispenser in the grey waiting room and arranged them on top of the grey cupboard.

She put her shapeless bag on the grey vinyl covered foam padded chair beside the bed, and not wanting to be bothered with overly cheerful bustling nurses, shut the door.

The grey curtains around the bed were closed, as were the room dividing curtains and the windows curtains.

Way too much grey.

Susan's poor, emaciated, corpse like body, clad in a grey hospital gown, was a mass of cheery red, blue and green wires and tubes hooked up to beeping machines.

This, Agatha knew, was not the way Susan had wanted to go.

Susan had looked forward to dying naturally.

Ideally on a park bench in some lovely gardens; tall gum trees, riotous flowers, and lots of bright chirping parrots.

Perhaps somewhere near a lake or river.

Somewhere tranquil and relaxing where she could lay her earthly worries aside before calmly moving on to whatever happened next.

Too late for that now.

"I'll just open up the windows and let some air in here shall I?" asked Agatha as she pulled back the curtains, and opened the window as wide as it would go to let the sunshine and clean fresh smell of warm eucalyptus into the room.

"You're not any better I see," she said as she ferreted out a couple of coins and laid them one at a time on Susan's eyelids, then sat next to the bed.

Susan of course said nothing, but Agatha took her hand and put herself in Susan's memory, which was about all that was left of her.

"Ah, you're back," Susan said.

Her memory place was very like the place she'd hoped to die in.

Agatha sat on the park bench next to her, "I am. I thought it was only fair to offer you one last chance."

Susan laughed. "No, I'm good. It's done now anyway.

"Still Mummy's little soldier?"

Susan reached over to pat her hand, and Agatha stiffened, before relaxing.

"Perhaps my next life will be better."

Agatha smiled, she hadn't expected any different, "I'll make sure of it."

They sat in silence, watching the wind in the trees and listening to the birds and insects.

"You know, you've been my most constant friend," Susan said.

"I can't be your friend, I'm not human."

Susan smiled, "yet whenever things felt the worse, there you were."

"I'd hardly call three times over your lifetime constant."

"Do you remember the first time we met?"

"I do, I even had the idea at the time you were an unusual girl."

«« • »»

Susan was in some kind of dormitory, not exactly sure why, not exactly sure where. She thought she was in a Victorian basement.

The room was small, with filthy walls and floor.

There were six beds in the room, but the scary nurse had closed the creaking door with a solid thud, leaving her all alone.

There were no windows, only two old fashioned fluorescent bar lights hanging from the ceiling.

Which was low and covered with large, dented black painted pipes, suspended from the ceiling with steel ties. Also painted black.

She lay in bed, the covers pulled up high to her neck, fingers tightly linked together under-neath them, looking up at a large dark stain on the ceiling.

It might have been mould or perhaps something worse.

Or maybe it was some kind of supernatural creature.

The closest light was flickering such that it seemed to be slithering across the ceiling.

Susan really wanted to call the nurse, but if anything, she was even more frightening than the thing on the ceiling.

She didn't think it was possible to be any more tense, until the door opened with a screech.

As her heart pounded, Susan thought she might die of fear until a cheery voice called out, "anyone home?"

At which point she got curious, released the choke hold on her fingers and sat up, "I'm home."

A woman was standing in the door way. Or at least Susan assumed it was a woman as she wasn't much more than a female shadow.

"Goodness, look at those lights," the woman said smashing the wall once with the flat or her fist. The light flickered for another few seconds, then shone on brighter than before.

It was an old woman wearing a white dress like a nurse, but different. Though Susan couldn't exactly pinpoint what the difference was.

"Are you all right in here Susan?" she asked.

"I haven't had any supper, is there anything to eat in here?"

"Ah, no, I'm sorry," the old woman said, "you've arrived too late for that, though I could rustle up a cup of tea and some biscuits."

"I would appreciate that," Susan said gravely.

The woman sat down on a chair next to her bed, reached into a shapeless bag Susan hadn't noticed, and pulled out a thermos and a packet of chocolate coated digestives.

She opened the packet and laid them on the bed before Susan, who waited to be invited to take one, while she undid the lid of the thermos and poured the hot tea into it.

She blew a little on it to cool it down before handing it over to Susan. "Please help yourself," she nudged the biscuit packet a little closer.

Susan closed her eyes and bowed her head and said, "For what we are about to receive, may the Lord make us truly thankful. For ever and ever. Amen."

"Amen," the old woman echoed.

Susan took a sip from her tea, then picked one biscuit from the plastic tray.

It looked enormous in her small hand.

Forgetting about the old woman for a mo-ment, she nibbled the biscuit, trying to make it last.

"I like digestives, don't you?" the old woman said.

"Yes, I do too. They help your digestion after dinner you know."

"I'd heard that."

"My name's Susan, what's yours?"

"Agatha."

"That's unusual, what does it mean?"

"Kind, or good."

"That's a good name."

"It used to be Atropos, which means inevitable, but I didn't like that so I changed it."

"I can understand that. But my mother gave me this name, so I'm not sure I could change it."

"She might not mind," said Agatha. "She might think a new name would suit you better now you've grown up."

"That's true. But I can't ask her, she died when I was born."

"How very sad," said Agatha.

"Yes, but I like to think she gave me all that she had. Besides my life I mean.

"I expect she's in heaven looking down on me, and I don't want to disappoint her."

"What if you could have a new Mummy? One who was alive."

Susan thought about it for a long time.

So long that she finished the tea and nibbled another two biscuits down to the crumbs.

"I'd have to say no. I'm not sure she'd like it if I gave up on her just because I hadn't met her."

"I see."

Susan nodded her head emphatically, "it's like that other nurse said, I'm Mummy's little soldier. So I'll soldier on through whatever comes toward me. And I'll battle to become a woman who would make my mother proud."

"It won't be easy."

"Then when it gets hard, I'll swallow my tears and keep marching on."

"Definitely Mummy's little soldier," Agatha dabbed her eyes with a big blue polka-dotted handkerchief.

"I tell you what," she said rummaging in her bag again, "I've got a lovely book to help you through," and she pulled out a small hardback, "it's a sad story about some luckless children," and gave it to Susan.

"Thank you," she said.

"Grow up big and strong," Agatha said as she put the thermos pieces together, and back into the bag, "and make your mother proud.

"Now I must be away, so you keep the biscuits hidden or that nurse will confiscate them."

Susan watched her leave, and only once she was sure Agatha was gone, did she turn the book over and open it up. The first page had her name written in handwriting very much like hers.

She glanced up at the stain, and was relieved to see it was just a stain. As if one of the pipes had burst a long time ago.

«« • »»

Susan laughed, "my goodness, what a precocious brat! I wonder you could stand me."

Agatha smiled, "you were so brave that first night in the orphanage, I had to keep track of you as the time passed by."

"I'm not entirely sure I got any better."

"I don't know, it may seem an ordinary life to you, but others found you inspiring."

Susan snorted.

"It's true! Generally, people assume it's their destiny to be happy, healthy and wealthy, but it's people like you who make the most of their lives.

"And you're almost always happier."

Susan smiled, "I suppose I got to almost everything I wanted to."

"Do you remember the second time we met?"

《《 • 》》

Susan pulled a handkerchief from her pocket, gave the wooden seat a quick flick to clean it, then sat on it to rest.

She tucked her backpack between her legs, took a sip of her take away coffee, and paused to read the graffiti on the chair.

For a so-called elite university, it was disappointingly common.

Jeremy loves Jason, she read.

Frida sucks balls.

Mr Singer is an imperialist.

At this level she'd hoped to find searing critiques of the patriarchy.

Or philosophical positions.

Or just something witty.

Then again, as always, graffiti calls to our most basic needs, so good on Frida.

Always assuming she did indeed suck balls, and the statement wasn't libellous.

And she rather though that perhaps Mr Singer might be a fascist rather than an imperialist.

Unless, of course, he'd travelled here with an Emperor from an alternate universe to overthrow the democratically elected government.

She pulled her favourite soft green cardigan more closely around her.

The gentle breeze was so gentle that most people wouldn't have noticed it, though for Susan it cut deeply through the fine weave.

But, being her first day, she'd wanted to look pretty rather than practical.

There would be plenty of other days to be practical.

Though she was wearing her fine gauge silk Long Johns beneath her blue jeans and a camisole under her t-shirt, and thick woollen socks under her fashionably chunky boots.

The seat she was sitting on was in the quadrangle, which might once have been laid to lawn, but the volume of students passing from building to building had rendered it to dirt and ground up bits of plastic packaging.

She watched the students, hoping a little, someone might take a seat next to her and start talking.

Though she'd planned her charm assault for class.

The quadrangle contained one stunted tree, that received so little light or rain, it was little more than a stick with a leaf on it.

If a bird happened to sit on it, it would collapse under the weight.

Being stunted herself, she felt sorry for the tree, and wanted to set it up with a solar light and automatic sprinkler.

Perhaps it was there as a lesson to the hale and hearty to enjoy their physicality while they could.

She'd heard the original tree, planted when the original, smaller buildings were new, had been struck by lightning.

Perhaps the lesson there was for people like her; enjoy your time while it lasts.

And Susan had every intention of sucking the marrow while she could.

As far as she could go.

Which according to her medical team's predictions, wasn't even long enough to finish university.

Just being there among the young people who hadn't really started living yet, was enough.

In the midst of the scattered, multicoloured groups of chattering students, she felt as though she might live forever.

As though she had all the time in the world.

She looked up and around at the Gothic sandstone building surrounding the quadrangle, trying to orient herself, though the signs were too small for her to read from her seat.

The buildings contained the Library, Arts, Electrical Engineering, and the Wilson Hall; named after Edward Wilson the actor, and used by theatre arts students for live performances.

Her target was Arts, and she gambled the building with the artistic carvings of gargoyles and other creatures was the arts building rather than the library or the theatre.

She couldn't imagine engineering as anything other than the plain one with mullioned win-dows.

She was just getting up when a boy backed into her, knocking her to the ground.

According to the TV shows, he should have immediately turned around to see if she was okay, and then fallen deeply in love with her.

In actuality, he didn't even notice.

She sat on the ground, watching him walk away with his two friends.

That she could not shoot fire from her eyes was surely a miracle, because if she could, those guys would be meat milkshakes splattered across the quadrangle.

She shook her head and started to get up when a hand appeared out of nowhere.

Susan looked up at the owner, a girl with a shaved head, a face full of piercings, and a set of large red headphones.

The girl curled her fingers back into her palm three times, and after a pause did it again.

Only then did Susan realise she was offering a hand up.

Susan reached out towards her, and the girl grabbed her wrist and pulled her up.

"Thanks."

"No worries," the girl said and started walking away.

"Wait," the girl looked back over her shoulder, "what's your name?"

A smile lit up her face, "Grace," she said, and kept walking.

After a moment spent watching her back getting smaller, Susan hefted her backpack, and re-gretfully walked in the direction of the fancy building.

Which turned out to be the library.

Still, the campus bookshop was in the ground floor east, and she needed to see if some of her textbooks had come back into stock.

There was rather a large line of people waiting for attention, but they seemed to be moving along reasonably fast.

She checked her watch and decided she'd wait for ten minutes then try for the Arts building.

As she got nearer the front of the queue, she noticed a strangely familiar old lady working there.

She almost remembered the name, and by the time she's got to the front of the queue she though she had it.

"What can I help you with?" the woman asked.

"Agatha?"

The woman looked at Susan for so long she thought she must have been mistaken.

Then she took a deep breath and said, "how do you know my name."

"On my first day at the orphanage you stopped by my bed with tea and chocolate digestives. And a book."

"So you... recognised me?"

"Yes!"

"That's not possible."

"You didn't stop by my bed?"

"Are you sure it was me?"

"Of course. You haven't aged a day. Literally. Haven't changed at all."

"You shouldn't be able see me. No one sees me as I am."

"Don't you remember me?"

"Of course, you're Mummy's little soldier.'

"That's right," said Susan. "I seem to recall you offered me a new Mummy."

"And I can see you grew up well. Your mother would be pleased you got into a university. Especially this one."

"I did it for you too. Even though Nurse Lambert tried to convince me I'd dreamed you, but I wanted to make you proud. Just in case I met you again."

"What about your first love? Would you change that now?"

Susan smiled, "I haven't met her yet, how could I change her for someone else without giving her a chance?"

Agatha nodded as if it all made sense to her now, "and are you still swallowing your tears?"

Susan looked away, but nodded.

"You'll want to see someone for that. And better sooner than later.

"Now," Agatha slid some books into a paper bag and pulled the handles out, "here are the books you have on hold, and I've slipped in a story about young love. That'll be $34.75."

Susan handed over cash, crumpled her change into the pocket of her jeans, and took the bag.

"Thank you for inspiring me to keep going every day. I hope that next time I see you, I've achieved something remarkable."

"You don't know it, but you already have."

Susan raised the bag in salute, and turned away.

Almost immediately she turned back, but the woman serving the next person wasn't Agatha.

Susan looked around for her, but she was nowhere to be seen.

Checking her watch and realised she was going to be late for class, and ran across the quadrangle to the building with alternating red and yellow bricks, to find it was the arts building.

Up two flights of stairs, the wrong way down the corridor, then back again to room 302.

And the first person she saw when she walked in the door was Grace.

《《 • 》》

Susan smiled, "ah yes, that day was a big day - meeting you again, then meeting my first love."

"I'm sorry it didn't work out."

"Did you have anything to do with that?"

"Not me, I only do the future. My sister does the present."

Susan turned towards Agatha, "all this time you have a sister and you didn't mention her?"

"Two actually, past and present."

"The past? What does she do?"

Agatha smiled, "weaving mostly. She decides what you remember and what you don't."

"Makes sense. I wish she'd let me forget Grace."

"Too many memories for her to take."

"Do you remember when Grace broke up with me?"

"I'm not sure I could forget that any more than you could."

《《 • 》》

Susan sat at the bus stop outside the red brick Victorian hospital's main entrance. Hands in her pockets, coat buttoned up to her chin, but she still felt cold.

Colder than normal.

She now knew when she was going to die.

Not the exact date of course, but that she had about three months left.

The road outside the hospital was packed with people coming and going; patients sneaking out for a quick ciggie, visitors arriving with gifts, and discharged patients slowly and carefully walking to cars ready to whisk them back to their normal lives.

Susan didn't see them.

She barely noticed the way the surrounding buildings blocked the wind, trapping the exhaust fumes and noise within the space.

The smell of hospital lingered on her clothes, and as she took a deep, steadying breath she caught notes of antiseptic, coffee, and air-conditioning.

Three months.

She swallowed the tears threatening to rain down her face, then laughed at herself.

Agatha had been right. She should have seen someone for it, and now with twenty years gone by, it was too late.

Though how could an eighteen-year-old know or care about the future.

She, like every other child in a grown-up's body, had assumed she was immortal.

She swallowed again.

And now she knew she wasn't.

There were so many things she'd need to do to get her affairs in order, but today...

She needed a day to eat junk food, drink wine, and snuggle up with Grace to watch horror movies.

To pretend everything was normal.

On which note, where was Grace?

She pulled her phone out of her pocket and saw she had a voice mail.

> *Hi Susan. It's me.*
>
> *Look... I, um, I met someone.*
>
> *And I know you're going through a hard time right now.*
>
> *But I just can't stand to watch you die.*
>
> *And by the time you get home I'll be gone.*
>
> *I've got a new phone so don't try to call me.*
>
> *We're moving interstate, so don't look for me either.*

I, er. I hope you get better.

I.

I.

Take care of yourself.

Susan swallowed.

And listened to the message again.

And again.

And again.

She was about to listen to it one more, when a voice said, "don't. It won't change anything."

She looked up to see Agatha, eyes full of sympathy. Agatha sat down, clasping a shapeless bag in her lap.

"I suppose I should listen to you this time." Her voice wobbled, and she swallowed again."

"You've nothing to lose by letting the tears out now," Agatha said.

A bus paused at the stop, and Agatha waved it on.

"I suppose not, but it's habit now"

They sat in silence, and after a time Agatha waved another bus on.

"So. What do I do now?"

"Well, unless you want to swap lives at this stage, you just carry on."

Susan grinned a little nastily, "should I swap mine for Grace's?"

"If that's what you want."

Susan sighed. "No, I've come this far. And it wouldn't be fair to let a stranger take it the last three months."

"I wish I could tell you it will all be okay, but we both know it won't."

"How could it be when my body is destroying itself. I suppose all those bitter tears have been eating it away all this time."

"Or maybe it's just the cumulation of all those choices you thought were small and didn't matter in the long run."

"Maybe."

Agatha let the silence draw out.

Susan sighed, then swallowed, then laughed.

"I really don't want to do this." She looked up at Agatha, "can't you do something?"

"I offered you a new life. For the third time I might add - most people don't get a single offer."

"No. I mean help with the pain or something."

"That's what the pills in your pocket are for."

"The ones that make me feel ill and sleepy you mean."

Agatha shrugged, "there's no doubt it's a hard choice."

"I should go home, but without Grace..."

Agatha smiled grimly, "I suppose if nothing else she's taken herself off your to do list. And harsh as you might think it, and hard as it may be to do it on your own, you don't have to be brave for her. You can be your own little soldier."

The ghost of a smile flitted across Susan's face as she swallowed, "I suppose you're right about that. I did always try to minimise the impact on her."

"It's funny in a way, that she seemed so strong the first day, but turned out to be so weak," Agatha said.

Susan stiffened, but had to concede that Grace had always been weak. Though she'd made Susan stronger and more capable, shaping her as the protector from life's nastiness.

And it was true that she couldn't be strong for anyone else, let alone herself anymore.

"You wouldn't fancy some ramen with a bucket of saké would you?"

"Ah, as fun as that would be, I have an ap-pointment.

"Another person with an unfortunate fate?"

Agatha laughed, "not this time - family dinner. You've no idea how lucky you are to be alone."

"I always thought family were a source of strength."

"Some families maybe, mine, not so much. Claudia always gets drunk and maudlin, and Laura's always busy fielding phone calls and get-ting texts."

"I guess everyone has their own problems."

"Do what you were planning to do; eat junk food, get shit faced and watch horror movies. To-morrow is plenty of time to write your bucket list."

"I will."

"Ah, I've got a book for you," she rooted around in the bag and handed it to Susan, "it's a story about a ghost that can't let go."

"I appreciate the humour in your choices."

Agatha stood up, "I'll see you again soon."

«« • »»

"Did you bring me another book?" Susan asked.

"Not this time. You've passed the need for books."

They sat in silence for a while, then Susan asked, "will it hurt?"

"Not your body, but maybe your mind will re-sist."

"I'm at ease. I had enough time to get every-thing done."

"Well done," said Agatha.

As they watched, a funeral barge approached, and they stood to receive it.

"Will it take long?"

Agatha assessed Susan's fading, wavering form, "you've already begun."

"Any last hints or instructions?"

"I can't follow where you're going."

Susan walked towards the boat and stepped inside it. "Thank you for coming to me. I hope you won't miss me too much."

And with that, the last remains of Susan and the boat dissipated and Agatha was alone.

As Susan's memory collapsed around her, Agatha was ejected back into her body.

She sighed and let Susan's hand go. If only all people were as content with their lives as Susan.

The coins were gone, and she nodded with satisfaction.

She picked up her bag and rummaged around inside for an apple.

No time to rest, it was time for her next client.

THE END

As a small token of my thanks for reading...

Please enjoy 10% off everything (excluding shipping)

at alexandriablaelock.com

with the code susanten.

Turn the page for some ideas where to use it,

Life interrupted

To say the letter was a surprise was an understatement. It arrived addressed to Miss Finlay Cox, which made the contents even more extraordinary.

Orphan Finn Cox inherits a cottage. Thinks it holds the key to her origins. Of course she takes a look. Who wouldn't?

But when she gets there, she gets more than she bargained for.

Is it friend, family or foe?

All she wants is a place of her own.

When Alison Porter finds a tiny cottage for sale, she thinks her dreams have come true. Inside virgin bushland, "Crow Cottage" sits on the smallest parcel of cleared land.

It's old. It's run down. It's keeping a secret.

Stumbling through a mysterious portal in the garden, she finds herself in a place of mystery and intrigue. As the past, present and future collide, she must unravel the secret, for only then can she reweave the tapestry of time.

If you love a story of twists and turns, where nothing is what it seems, grab Weaving the Wildwood today

Meet Morag Clementine. The new housekeeper at historic Hayward Hall.

Her practical and capable attitude usually keeps her out of trouble.

bove all, her no-nonsense, get it done approach. And her get in the middle of the scrum outlook. Just as well, because Hayward Hall needs someone like her.

In this genre-spanning collection of original stories, Morag finds herself ensnared in the History of Hayward Hall...

No ordinary housekeeper, can Morag save the house, one century at a time?

Perhaps you'll carry your new books
in one of these bags

Enjoy them while drinking from
one of these mugs

Or wearing one of these t-shirts

ABOUT THE AUTHOR

Australian author Alexandria Blaelock writes mostly fantasy and mystery.

She's appeared in the Stringybark Anthology *Crowd Surfing*, *Pulphouse Fiction Magazine*, and *Ellery Queen's Mystery Magazine*.

She's also written five self-help books applying business techniques to personal matters like getting dressed, tidying up, and feeding friends.

When not exploring parallel universes, she talks to animals, indulges in K-dramas, and sips Campari. She lives in the Dandenongs, where she relishes the sound of birdsong, the scent of gum leaves and the sun on her face.

Discover more at https://alexandriablaelock.com.

www.ingramcontent.com/pod-product-compliance
Lightning Source LLC
Chambersburg PA
CBHW051829180726
48283CB00004BA/1364